The Lost Treasure

Victorian stories linking with the History
National Curriculum.

First published in 1996 by Franklin Watts

This paperback edition published in 1997

Franklin Watts
96 Leonard Street
London EC2A 4RH

Franklin Watts Australia
14 Mars Road
Lane Cove
NSW 2006

Series editor: Paula Borton
Consultant: Joan Blyth
Designer: Kirstie Billingham

A CIP catalogue record for this book
is available from the British Library.

ISBN 0 7496 2635 6 (pbk)
0 7496 2375 6 (hbk)

Dewey Classification 941.081

Printed in Great Britain

The Lost Treasure

by
Mary Hooper

Illustrations by Lesley Bisseker

W

FRANKLIN WATTS
LONDON • NEW YORK • SYDNEY

1

The Adventure Begins

George's eyes were round as saucers as he gazed up at the soaring glass roof of the railway station, at the massive pillars and ironwork and arches. "It's like a great big church!"

"It's like being inside the Crystal

Palace!" Poppy said, staring around her.

In the big London station, all was bustle and noise and drama. Smartly dressed people paraded behind porters wheeling piles of leather luggage, steam from the engines hissed and billowed, uniformed men blew whistles and bellowed to each other across the platforms.

"I hope we won't get lost," George said with a shiver of fright. "I hope you know where you're going, our Poppy."

"Course I do," Poppy said. "Don't you trust your big sister? Didn't I rescue you from the Mill and all?"

Poppy and George were in London

because they'd been asked by their local
doctor to deliver some valuable books to a
friend of his in the City. They'd travelled
to London by train and were to stay one
night in a lodging house before returning
the next day.

Poppy looked down at the piece of paper she'd been given by the doctor. "We've got to take the books to a big office in a street near St Paul's Cathedral," she said to George, and as she said the last words a shiver of excitement ran through her. She had a reason of her own for wanting to do this errand...

Even without this, though, it was good to get away from home for a while. Although their brother Alfred, and the twins Lily and Rose, were at the Mill, that still left young Marigold, Daisy and baby Albert all at home and sharing a bedroom with Poppy and George. The house where

8

they lived with Ma and Dad was cramped and dingy and money was short, most nights they went to bed with nothing inside them but a crust of bread.

"What we're going to do," Poppy said, "is deliver the books as quickly as we can, then explore." She picked up one end of the canvas bag containing the precious books. "Come on, George. Let the adventure begin!"

Outside the station it was just as crowded. Omnibuses and coaches lined the road three deep around the station entrance, their horses pawing the ground.

Stalls had been set out all along the pavement selling hot potatoes, roast chestnuts, penny pies, spice-cakes, hot eels, muffins and all sorts of hot and cold drinks. Above the clamour, the stall-holders could be heard bellowing to the crowds of people, urging them to "Come buy!"

Poppy and George's mouths began to water but Poppy tugged at George to come away.

"We can't afford to buy any of this fancy stuff," she said. "After we pay for our lodgings tonight we've just got enough for a loaf of bread." She pulled him past the woman who was shouting about her "Luvverly hot pea soup!" and tried not to look at the warm gingerbread on the next stall.

"We'll find something to eat later," she said, "and nothing fancy, neither. Bread and lard is what we're used to and bread and lard is what we'll have!"

2

The Riddle

"St. Paul's Cathedral!" Poppy said, and both she and George stood on the wide steps and stared up at the huge and magnificent building before them.

Poppy shivered with excitement. "George," she said, "somewhere near here,

14

there's hidden treasure!"

"Is there really?" George said, clapping his hands. "Whose treasure is it?"

"Well," Poppy began, "a long, long time ago, Ma's family were very rich. One day there was an argument and Great-Grandmother was so annoyed about it that she hid her money away and told her four grown-up children that they'd only get hold of it if they made friends."

"And did they?" George asked excitedly.

Poppy shook her head. "She gave them each a piece of jewellery containing a golden key and one line of a riddle. If they got together and completed the riddle, then the secret hiding place of the treasure would be revealed."

"Tell me the riddle!" George begged.

"I've only got three lines so far," Poppy said, but she recited all the same –

"*When life's torch flames burn no more,
And the urn is covered o'er,
Where Hope waits, bowed
down with sorrow,*"

George frowned and shook his head, trying to make sense of it all.

"It doesn't mean much," Poppy said. "We need to have the last line."

"And is the treasure in here? In the Cathedral?" George asked, leaning back so far to look at the building that he almost fell over. "However will we find it?"

"It's not in here," Poppy said. "It's around

here somewhere. It could be anywhere."

"When life's torch flames burn no more..." George muttered to himself, shaking his head and frowning deeply.

He ran up the steps, dodging between the people, and started walking in and out of the marble pillars in front of the vast doors. As he walked he looked intently about him –

up and down, from right to left.

"Don't be daft!" Poppy called. "It's not going to be as obvious as that, is it? If it was, someone would have found it long ago.

"Oh, let's go in!" George called down to Poppy from the top of the steps.

"Not now," she said. "First we must get these books delivered. After that we —" She gave a sudden scream. "George, where's the bag?"

George stopped in his tracks. "We just put it on the steps there..." He pointed and they both stared. At nothing.

"It can't have just disappeared!" Poppy said frantically.

"I thought you were watching it!"

"I thought you were."

George ran down the steps and just
stared at the empty space. "It's gone all
right," he said. He looked around.
"Someone must have taken it."

Poppy burst into tears. "Oh George,
we're going to be in terrible trouble!" she cried.

No one seemed to want to help them.

There were so many children roaming the streets, so many waifs and strays, that most people Poppy approached just thought she was begging and brushed her off before she'd had a chance to speak. Eventually, though, someone told her to tell a policeman. Poppy had never even seen one of these uniformed persons before. They were so new and rare that it took most of the afternoon to find one, and, to her dismay, when he'd heard what she had to say he started laughing.

"That's a good one!" he said.
"You've had some valuable books stolen,
have you?"

"And our return tickets and our money
and everything!" George said.

"They were there one minute and gone
the next!"

"Are you sure you haven't sold the
books and spent the money!" the
policeman said with a grin. "That's what
I think has happened to them."

"No, we haven't!"
Poppy said indignantly.

"We wouldn't dare!"
said George.

"That's what you tell
me," the policeman said.
"Well, I expect it works
sometimes, but not with me. Now run
along home, both of you!"

"But we can't get home!" George said.
"Not without our tickets!"

"Then you'll just have to work to earn
some money, same as the others," said the
policeman. "It's no good you coming
begging from me. Be off with you!"

And with that he strode
away without a backward
glance, leaving Poppy and
George standing in the cold,
grey street without a
penny piece
between them.

3

Faith, Hope and Charity

It was getting dark and had started to snow. Both Poppy and George were tired – and hungry, too. Poppy kept wishing that she'd bought food earlier, when they'd been at the station. When she closed her eyes she could almost see the stall that had been selling gingerbread, practically sniff its warm, spicy fragrance.

But almost more pressing than the need to eat was the need to find somewhere to stay the night. In the dark shadows of buildings Poppy could see small huddles of homeless children gathering. Surely, though, she and George wouldn't have to sleep on the streets?

She knew there were hostels and shelters for the homeless, but where were they?

Poppy tried to ask passers-by, but everytime she did she was ignored or shouted at.

At last she stopped a grubby-looking boy wearing a tattered suit and strange headgear which might once have been a top hat.

"Excuse me," she asked politely, "but do you know of anywhere we could stay the night? I've heard there are shelters for the homeless."

The boy hooted with laughter. "Not now," he scoffed. "If you wanted somewhere, you should have started queuing at nine o'clock this morning."

George started to cry. "But I want to stop walking. I'm tired and I'm cold."

Poppy shushed him. "There must be somewhere," she said.

"Well," the boy said, "there's a few of us live in a house around the back of the Cathedral. It's not really for the likes of you – seeing as you look quite la-de-dah – but you're welcome to come along."

Poppy nudged George hard. "Stop that crying," she said. "What d'you think? Shall we go?"

"Suppose we'll have to," George said between sniffs.

Poppy did her best to smile at the boy, though her face was so cold it felt as if it were frozen. "Yes, please," she said. "We'd like to come with you."

"Off we go then!" said the boy. He took off his hat and flourished it. "They call me Topper on account of I always wears this hat," he said. "What are your names, and have you got any money?"

"I'm Poppy and this is George," Poppy said. "And we haven't got any money. None at all."

"Not even enough for a loaf of bread," put in George.

27

"Well, I can stand you a penny loaf," Topper said. "But you'd best think about earning some money of your own."

"How can I do that?" Poppy asked.

Topper looked her up and down. "You could sell that posh dress you're wearing, for a start."

Poppy shook her head. "My dress was given to me by the Honourable Isabella Throckmorten," she said proudly. "I saved her life at the Great Exhibition – when I was working for her father, Lord Throckmorten, you know."

Poppy had been working

as a scullery maid in the rich lord's big house when she'd heard about the awful conditions in his Mill. Her brothers and sisters were working there as apprentices and she'd gone to find them. Poppy discovered that George was injured, so she'd had to rescue him and take him home to Ma. Because of what she'd done, though, she'd lost her job.

"Lord Throckmorten – get you!" Topper said.

Poppy pulled a face. Life in the Throckmorten house hadn't been quite as good as it sounded...

"'Course, there's all sorts of other things you could do to get money," Topper went on. "You could sell matches or fruit or ribbons, or you could hold carriage doors open for the ladies and gents, or you could sweep the dirt out of their paths. You could be a mudlark, of course – same as I am."

"That sounds all right," Poppy said.
"How d'you be one of those?"

"Easy!" Topper said. "You wait until
low tide and then you go down on to

the river, in the mud, and pick up things."

"What sort of things?" Poppy asked, now noticing that Topper's legs were caked with mud and his clothes stained brown.

"All sorts. Anything that'll earn a penny or two – bits of coal, wood, rope, old bottles and nails, things washed up by the tide. You collect 'em and then you sell 'em."

"But isn't it freezing – standing in the mud?" George asked.

"'Tis that!" said Topper. "And sometimes you can be wading in the stuff all day and get froze right through and still not find a pennyworth."

"I don't fancy that," Poppy said, looking down at her good frock. "Maybe I'll try something else." Maybe, she thought, it's time to find the treasure...

Topper led them through a warren of
cobbled lanes and dark, narrow alleyways.
Then he took them into a vast cemetery in
which marble headstones gleamed
white in the moonlight.

"This is somewhere you could stay," he
said. "There's a few little gangs live here."

"In the cemetery?" George faltered.

"Course!" Topper said. "You've got

shelter in those big marble houses. You get
a little fire going and you're warm. And
you've got company, too. You've got
company from your mates and you've got
company from the angels!" he grinned,
pointing at the graceful marble figures at
the head of some of the graves.

"Some company!" George said.

"You've got these lovely ladies, too,"
Topper went on as they stopped in front
of three statues swirled around with

marble draperies. "All dressed in their best!
Poppy and George, meet Faith, Hope
and Charity."

"Are those their names?" George asked.

"Certainly," Topper said, and he
pulled off his tatty top hat and gave a deep

bow to the statues.

They walked on, stopping sometimes
to admire the most beautiful of the figures
or so that Poppy could read an inscription.
Topper, who couldn't even read his own
name, was highly taken with this.

When they came out of the gate at the
other end, Topper led them down a
narrow passageway and towards a shabby
row of buildings.

"Here we are – home!" he said proudly.

Poppy looked up at the
wreck before them and
pulled a face. The
row of houses,
or what was left
of them, leant
this way and that,
almost falling
in on themselves.

There were great holes in the plaster fronts and no house had any door to speak of.

"Is this where you live? Is this really your home?" Poppy asked after a moment.

"Indeed it is!" Topper said. "We're all mudlarks here – and you're very welcome to join us."

4

Earning Pennies

That first night – and every other night
they were there, come to that – Poppy and
George slept under nothing but old
newspapers. Because they were in a room
with eight other children, though, they
managed to keep fairly warm. It wasn't

too bad, but Poppy was desperate to get them both home as soon as she could. She had to earn money for their tickets first, though, and they also had to eat. There could be no better time, Poppy decided, for that treasure to be found...

The next morning, as soon as it was light, she borrowed a penny from Topper to buy some milk and a chunk of stale bread. She took it back to the house to share with George and then set out again to see how she might earn some money.

The snag, she soon discovered, was that you had to have money to spend before you could make any. You needed to buy a stock of matches before you could sell them again, or you had to buy cheap fruit or flowers from the market before you could sell them on to a passing lady. You even had to buy yourself a broom before you could go crossing-sweeping – brushing the ground free of mud, litter (and worse) so that a lady or gent could walk across the pavement from shop to carriage without soiling their clothes. Another way of making money was to put on a performance – singing or dancing, juggling or fortune-telling. Poppy knew, however, that she would be no good at any of those.

Later that day, after wandering around watching the other children, she decided that the simplest way she could earn a halfpenny was to stand in the doorway of a shop waiting to carry packages out to a carriage. There was a lot of competition for this. A whole patrol of children was working outside the store which Poppy chose, but because she was well-dressed in comparison to them, she did quite well. By the time the store closed that day she'd made, in pennies and half-pennies, seven pence.

This was enough for two pieces of hot fish in batter, which she carried home to George in triumph. If she could just get a little more money together, she thought, enough for food for two or three days, then she wouldn't have to spend all her time in shop doorways. Then they could start treasure hunting.

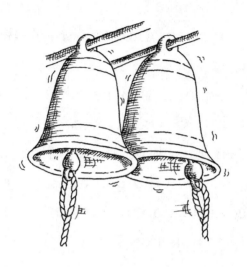

5

Quiet Streets

Three days later, Poppy and George woke to church bells. It sounded, she thought, as if they were pealing out all over the city.

"Where is everyone?" George suddenly asked, sitting bolt upright.

Poppy looked round. There were no

other children in the big, cold room of the mudlarks' house. Not even Topper. Come to think of it, she thought, she hadn't seen him the day before, either.

"D'you think they've all gone off to work early?" George asked.

"They must have done," Poppy said.

"How much did you make yesterday?" he asked, and Poppy counted out four pennies into his hand.

"Not enough to stop work today.

Do you feel all right to come out with me carrying packages?" she asked George, who'd not long recovered from his accident on the mill machines. "Perhaps if you put your sling back on the rich ladies might take pity on you."

George grumbled a bit while Poppy tied on his sling and, after eating a piece of bread each, they set out to walk to one of the big shopping areas.

It was snowing again but this time it was settling on the roads, covering the dirt

and litter with a frosty whiteness. It was settling, Poppy suddenly realised, because the streets were deserted. Why, though?

"Where is everyone?" George asked.

Poppy stopped, puzzled. "I don't know," she said.

They passed through the graveyard, the statues of Faith, Hope and Charity more beautiful than ever in the falling snow, and came to a square containing tall, elegant houses. All was quiet, there was only the

sound of nearby church bells ringing.

Poppy shook her head in bewilderment. "I don't think we'll make much money today," she said. "Folks don't seem to be coming out of their homes."

"Is it because of the weather?" George asked, and Poppy said she just couldn't make it out at all.

They crossed the square, but as they were about to pass the corner house they came to a sudden stop, gasping at the sight before them.

Through the big window they could see a fir tree, lit with dozens of tiny candles, bright with flags and small wooden figures, topped by a shining golden star.

"What's that?" George said in wonder.

Poppy gazed at the glorious sight. "They call that a Christmas tree," she breathed.

They looked further in, to a richly decorated room with a fire flaming in the hearth, and a family dressed in velvets and satins. At the other end of the room, two girls played with a dolls' house which was as tall as themselves, and a boy sat on a big wooden rocking horse.

"That's why there's no one around," Poppy said a little sadly. "Today is Christmas Day – and we didn't even know it!"

6

The Key

"I don't want to go back to where we live," George said when Poppy eventually got him away from the sight of the shimmering tree. "It's cold and it's dirty and it's awful."

"It's somewhere to stay until we earn

enough money to get home," Poppy said. "You wouldn't rather be out on the streets, would you?"

George shook his head. "S'pose not," he said. "But Poppy, I do wish we had more to eat and I wish we were warm." He suddenly looked fierce. "I want us to live in a house like that one. I want us to have a Christmas tree!"

"Look," Poppy said rather desperately. "I told you, one day we'll find the treasure, and then we'll have all the food and all the warmth we want.

And we'll have the biggest Christmas tree anyone's ever seen. As big as a house!"

But George didn't look as if he believed her, so Poppy, to cheer him up, said that they'd go into a tavern and ask to wash some glasses in return for a penny pie.

They walked a long way before they found one which was open. When they did, George sat on the dusty floor as near as he could to the few coals glowing in the fireplace, while Poppy queued up to talk to the landlord.

While she waited, she listened to two
women chatting about a funeral which
had taken place the day before.

"Proper lovely, it was," one of them
said. "Six horses with black plumes pulling
a glass carriage."

"And I hear he's having a beautiful
tomb," said the other. "No expense spared.
It's a granite slab with a big marble urn
on it – and an Italian sculptor is coming to
carve the draperies over it."

Poppy was thinking about meat pies, but when she heard what the woman said, all thoughts of eating went out of her head. Suddenly she was thinking about marble urns – and the line of the riddle, *And the urn is covered o'er...*

She clapped her hand to her mouth. Of course! That's where you found covered urns – as stone ornaments in churchyards! And, down-turned torches, too – *When life's torch flames burn no more...* Suddenly she gave a great scream of excitement which made the two women turn and stare at her. You found Hope in churchyards, too! She'd seen the figures of Faith, Hope and Charity in the graveyard only that morning. *Where Hope waits, bowed down with sorrow...*

She ran back to George and pulled him to his feet. He shook her off crossly. "Where's my pie?" he asked. "I'm starving!"

"We're not worrying about pies now," Poppy said.

"What?!"

"We've got other things to do."

"What d'you mean?"

"You and I, my boy," said Poppy, "are going treasure hunting!"

◆

Poppy and George stood shivering before the three marble figures.

Poppy shook her head. "It's no good," she said, "this can't be the right statue.

Hope isn't bowed down with sorrow – not like the riddle says."

"What?" George asked. "What are you talking about?"

"Hope – I've just worked it out. She's a person. Or nearly – she's a statue. So it must be in another churchyard!"

"What must?"

"The treasure!" Poppy said wildly.

"But I don't understand..."

"You will!" squealed Poppy over her shoulder. "Come on!"

"But I'm cold and I'm hungry," George said, tagging behind Poppy as she set off at a run through the falling snow.

"There are two more churchyards near St. Paul's," she said when they reached the street. "We've got to try and search them before it gets dark."

"Can't we eat first and—"

"No!" Poppy said. "We certainly can not!" A bit later, Poppy and George were standing in another cemetery beside a fancy tomb built to look like a little chapel. A stained glass window was set in the front of it, and underneath this was the statue of a woman, kneeling, head in hands.

HOPE

"Oh look," Poppy breathed. "It's Hope…"

"Is she bowed down with sorrow?" George asked with interest.

"I should say she is," Poppy said.

"And look," George went on, wandering round to the back of the chapel, "There's an urn here, covered over."

"And a down-turned torch!" Poppy yelled. "All the things in the riddle are here!

"Except the last line," put in George.

Poppy bit her lip, wondering. Then she stepped over the small iron railing which ran round the "chapel" and went right up to the front of it. What she saw there almost made her scream with excitement.

Behind the bowed figure of Hope, and hidden away from the casual passer-by, a small wooden door had been set into the stonework. It bore a brass plate which said – *Where life's torch flames*

burn no more
*   And the urn*
is covered o'er
*   Where*
Hope waits
bowed down
with sorrow
*   Seek within*
a bright
tomorrow

When life's torch flames burn no more,
And the urn is covered o'er,
Where Hope waits bowed down with sorrow,
Seek within a bright tomorrow

And then Poppy did scream. "Seek within a bright tomorrow!" she shrieked to George. "It's the last line of the riddle!"

"But what...but how...?" George stuttered.

"And there's a keyhole and..." she clutched at the piece of string round her neck and pulled out the golden key – the key she'd been wearing since she'd got the first line of the riddle.

She closed her eyes and wished. And
then she opened them and
put the key in the lock.

The key fitted.

The key turned.

The small wooden door
swung open.

"Oh, George," Poppy breathed,
and for a long, long moment the two
of them just stood there, snow falling around,
almost turned to statues themselves.

Then Poppy took a deep breath, put
her hand in the door and pulled out a
small wooden chest. When
she lifted the lid they
were almost dazzled by
the brightness of the
jewels inside.

Poppy was
quiet for

another long moment, and then she said softly, "It's over, George. We've found it. We'll take this home to Ma and Dad and we'll never, never be hungry again."

"Really?" George said. "And can we have a big house and a carriage and horses and a Christmas tree?"

Poppy nodded. "All those things."

"And can I have that meat pie now?" George asked.

"I should say so," said Poppy, and together they went out of the churchyard and towards their bright tomorrow...

Victorian life

Railways

The first railway, from Liverpool to Manchester, was completed in 1830. By the time Poppy came to London, in this story, the railways had spread all over the country. Thousands of men (like Poppy's Dad) were employed by the railway companies to help build the network. The big new London stations were very grand.

Homeless people

When people were poor in Victorian times they *were* really poor. They lived in the meanest coldest places and were often unable to feed themselves and their families. Because of this the streets were swarming with unwanted children who were dirty, ragged hungry and neglected. Doctor Barnardo was the first to do something about this. he started a ragged school for poor children and, in 1870, opened his first Home. The scheme grew and grew until 7,000 homeless children were housed under his care.

Christmas

Christmas as we know it, with cards and presents and a decorated, lit Christmas tree really started when Prince Albert (Queen Victoria's German husband) introduced English people to the customs of Germany. Only the rich could afford to celebrate it properly, of course, but it was an opportunity for the wealthiest of them to show, one day a year, how generous they could be. If Poppy and George, outside in the cold, had been seen by the happy family within, they might have been invited to join them.

Life on the Streets of London

In all the big cities, the streets were teeming with people trying to earn money. As well as grubbing in the mud for odds and ends, people worked on the rubbish dumps and even in sewers, trying to make money out of things that other people had thrown away. Some had stalls which sold fast food – hot eels, baked potatoes, meat pies, plum pudding, fried fish and sheeps' trotters, while some sold things they had made. Others scraped a living as street performers – dancers, puppeteers, acrobats, dancers and musicians.